Can I Play, Too?

by

K. Scott Conover

Proctor Publications • *Ann Arbor* • *Michigan* • *USA*

Proctor Publications
P.O. Box 2498
Ann Arbor, Michigan 48106
(800) 343–3034

Printed in the United States of America

Publisher's Cataloging-in-Publication
(Provided by Quality Books, Inc.)

Conover, K. Scott.
 Can I play, too? / K. Scott Conover. -- 1st ed.
 p. cm.
 SUMMARY: A young boy with orthopedic braces moves into a new
neighborhood, and finds it difficult to convince his peers to include him in
their games, but his courage leads him to basketball success and true friendship.
 Preassigned LCCN: 98-67942
 ISBN: 1-882792-69-6

 1. Physically handicapped children--Recreation--Juvenile fiction.
2. Orthopedic braces--Juvenile fiction. 3. Playmates--Juvenile fiction.
4. Basketball for children--Juvenile fiction. I. Title

PZ7.C76465Ca 1998   [Fic]
                                     QBI98-1337

This book is dedicated to God for the talents given to me, to my mother for her continuous support and inspiration and to my nephew for a successful future.

Preface

From the first day he started walking to the day he moved into a new neighborhood, Teddy encounters people who view and treat him differently. His innocent quest to *"play too"* leads him into adventures that teach him valuable lessons. His courage leads him to success and a deep understanding of the meaning of true friendship.

Chapter 1

A loud cry that is familiar to many hospitals filled Room 219 during the first evening hour.

"We have ourselves a strong, healthy boy," the doctor announced to the assisting nurses.

Indeed, the newborn baby was very strong and healthy; he weighed nearly ten pounds and had a cry as loud as a trumpet.

After performing a routine examination, the doctor handed the crying baby to his mother. Mrs. Watts, who was very exhausted, gently wrapped her arms around her son. She gave him a huge smile and a kiss on his small, round head, which was already covered with dark, curly hair.

"I want everyone to meet Theodore," said Mrs. Watts with a pride only a mother could know, acquainting the doctor and nurses with her son's name.

Carefully, Mrs. Watts counted the fingers and toes

on Theodore's hands and feet. Then she handed him over to the nurses to be bathed and clothed. Not purposely, Mrs. Watts fell into a deep sleep before the nurses could finish either task.

Two days later, Theodore Watts went for his first ride home in a taxicab. The day was extremely sunny and exceptionally hot. It was the last week in September which meant that the fall season had just started. The fall season was busy, being the time of year when children went back to school and farmers picked plump, red, juicy apples from the orchards. The leaves on the many trees in the neighborhood were beginning their colorful change and small animals gathered food to store, preparing for the long winter ahead.

Although the fall season brought about these wonderful activities, it could not bring back the one thing that Theodore would dearly miss. Earlier that year, Theodore's father left home. Left behind were Theodore's mother and two sisters, Loran and Magi. Now with his father away, Theodore would have to be the man of the house. But, with a half empty bottle of baby milk in his mouth, Theodore didn't appear to be ready for the title quite yet. Nevertheless, his mother sat quietly as she held her new born son close to her during the lonely taxicab ride home.

After driving through town and down a few blocks, the cab driver turned onto a dead end street. Proceeding slowly, the driver looked for house numbered 33. The house would be easy to locate because it was the only brown house on the street. In addition to being brown, the house was old and had a dirty wooden porch that led up to a sturdy gray door. On either side of the door were glass windows covered by white laced curtains. Inside, awaiting for Theodore's arrival were his aunt and two sisters.

Locating number 33 on the brown house, the driver made a u-turn and parked directly in front.

"That will be six dollars even, ma'am," the driver said in a loud voice.

The driver's voice awakened Theodore, who started crying and kicking in his mother's arms. Theodore made it extremely hard for his mother to reach into her black vinyl purse for the six dollars.

As his mother retrieved the money from her purse, Theodore's two sisters slammed open the door and raced down the porch stairs toward the taxicab.

During the race, Loran, who was ten years old, and the older of the two girls, exclaimed, "I'm goin' to see 'em first!"

Because Magi was anxious to see Theodore as well, she replied, "Mommy said I can see 'em first 'cause I'm still her baby, too!"

Magi was stretching the truth about being a baby because she had already turned eight years old during the middle part of June.

The truth was that neither of the girls wanted to be last, so each ran as fast as she could.

When Loran and Magi reached the taxicab, they were out of breath. Loran pushed Magi aside and quickly opened the car door for her mother.

"Hello, girls," greeted their mother.

Neither Loran nor Magi could reply because each was still trying to catch her breath. Instead, their attentions were directed toward Theodore, who appeared to be invisible because he was securely wrapped in warm blankets.

Safely inside the house, Theodore's mother unwrapped the blankets and placed him in the refurbished hand-carved wooden crib that had been in the family for many generations. Within a couple of seconds Theodore dropped off into one of his many afternoon naps.

After making sure Theodore was soundly asleep, his mother walked away from the crib and into the kitchen to make lunch. Loran and Magi, who were standing in their mother's shadow, crept up closely to the crib. They wanted to get a good look at

Theodore.

"Aw, ain't him cute?" Magi whispered as she looked at her little brother. Magi felt very proud to see Theodore. In fact, having a baby brother meant that she was no longer the youngest. That was nice because she always wanted to be an older sister. However, Magi would always be reminded by Loran who was the oldest.

"Only I can hold 'em, cause I'm the oldest," Loran uttered into Magi's ear.

Disagreeing with Loran's remarks, Magi yelled, "I can hold 'em, too!"

"No, you can't!" replied Loran.

"Yes, I can!" cried Magi.

"No, no, no!" Loran commanded.

"I can! I can!! I can!!" Magi shouted her final words.

At that point, Loran and Magi stopped arguing and began pushing and shoving each other. When the pushing and shoving was not enough, they wrestled each other to the floor.

Awakened by the noise in the room, Theodore let out a loud cry, startling his two sisters. Instantly, Loran and Magi stopped wrestling, scrambled back up to the crib and gave Theodore a blank look because they thought there was something wrong with him.

But the cry was simply a way for Theodore to let them know that after his short nap it was now time for his usual afternoon feeding.

Chapter 2

Theodore Watts was slow in learning how to walk and didn't start until he was nearly two years old. And even so, walking was very difficult for him. Often when Theodore tried walking, he would stumble and fall over his own feet. The falls left him with many bumps and bruises on his legs. In addition to stumbling and falling, Theodore's walk resembled that of a clumsy little bear cub. Therefore, amused by his unusual walking style, Theodore's mother gave him the nickname *Teddy*.

This nickname suited Theodore well, not just because Teddy was the usual nickname for the name Theodore, but it also referred to a lovable toy bear.

But after another year, when Teddy's walking problem still existed, his mother became very concerned. She decided to take Teddy to see Dr. Crisby. That brought about another problem. Teddy didn't like going to see Dr. Crisby because during his last visit, he got a shot in his rear end which ached for an entire week.

Teddy hid under the bed from his mother when it was time to go to the doctor's office. To get Teddy out of hiding, his mother knew she needed to tell him something to ease his mind.

"Nurse Sharon is waiting to see you," she said, knowing that Teddy had a small crush on Nurse Sharon.

"Okay, Mommy!" Teddy replied.

Another reason Teddy liked seeing Nurse Sharon was because she gave him a red lollipop during each of his visits. The sweet taste of a red lollipop always eased Teddy's fear.

When Teddy and his mother arrived at Dr. Crisby's office, they were greeted by a receptionist who directed them to the examination room. There, Teddy and his mother waited patiently for the doctor and nurse to arrive. Teddy sat on the hard cushioned examination table, fearful of getting yet another painful shot.

"Mommy, it won't hurt, right?" he asked with a look of fright on his face.

"Dr. Crisby won't hurt you because he's your friend, Teddy," his mother replied as she rubbed the

top of his head.

Teddy then sighed and placed his hands over his eyes, hoping that it would make him invisible.

"Nurse Sharon could hold your hand, too," his mother added, hoping to remove any fear that Teddy was feeling.

Since the thought of seeing Nurse Sharon sounded quite nice, Teddy returned his mother's gesture with a huge smile that showed he was missing his two front teeth.

At that moment, Dr. Crisby and Nurse Sharon walked into the examination room. Dr. Crisby was a tall, bald-headed gentleman. He was wearing his usual white jacket that covered a brown tie and navy blue trousers. His hands were always cold and smelled like soap.

Nurse Sharon was a middle-aged woman who looked liked she was in her late twenties. Her long hair went halfway down her white dress. Her hands were always soft and smelled like fresh spring flowers.

"Good morning, and how's my little Teddy bear doing today?" Dr. Crisby asked.

"Fine," Teddy said, as he tried to imitate Dr. Crisby's deep voice.

Teddy then hid behind his mother, fearing that he was about to get the dreadful shot.

"I have a nice red lollipop for Teddy when he gets finished," Nurse Sharon said in her usual sweet tone.

Conceding to Nurse Sharon's offer, Teddy came out of hiding and allowed Dr. Crisby to examine him.

After learning that Teddy's clumsy walk was due to his legs that had grown very crooked and weak, Dr. Crisby recommended that Teddy wear braces. The braces would give Teddy's legs strong support and help him walk properly.

Since Teddy's mother wanted his clumsy walk to be corrected, she allowed Dr. Crisby to place a pair of new, shiny, cold, steel-framed braces on Teddy's stubby legs. With the braces on his legs, Teddy took a few steps.

Clickety-click. Clickety-click.

The braces made a clicking sound as he tried walking slowly and cautiously. In addition to making a clicking sound, the braces made Teddy look even clumsier. Instead of looking like a clumsy bear cub, he now looked like a fish out of water. Seeing that Teddy was having a very difficult time walking in his new braces, Nurse Sharon gave him a smile and a handful of red lollipops instead of his usual single one.

Determined to get accustomed to the new braces,

Teddy walked a few times around the examination room. Then he and his mother said, "Good-bye," and left Dr. Crisby's office for their long walk home.

After walking only a couple of blocks, Teddy became exhausted. His legs were simply too weary to go much further. Therefore, he stopped and allowed his mother to place him on her back for the remainder of the way. Not minding the piggyback ride home, Teddy gave his mother a sticky kiss on her cheek and wrapped his arms around her neck.

Chapter 3

Over the next few months, Teddy continued to have a difficult time walking with his braces. Most of the time, he remained sitting in his bed while his two sisters read books to him. He wanted to eliminate having to walk. He also stayed inside the house to hide his braces from the other children in the neighborhood.

However, shortly after Teddy turned four years old, he became very comfortable walking with the braces on his legs. Not only did he feel comfortable walking, he ran and skipped. As a result, these accomplishments that would be quite simple to any four year old made Teddy feel very good about himself.

Rather than spending anymore of his time in the house listening to his sisters read books, Teddy wanted to play outside. He was finally ready to stop hiding his braces from the other children who loved to play in the fun area each Saturday. The fun area was a place on Teddy's dead end street that was safe for the children to play because it was blocked off with detour barriers to prohibit any traffic.

On the second Saturday in October, after eating breakfast, Teddy hurried to brush his teeth and change out of his pajamas and into his play clothes, a lightweight jacket and a red baseball cap. He then sat in front of the window that overlooked the neighborhood. Teddy stared out the window, waiting for the other children to gather outside and play their usual games like tag, dodge ball or duck-duck-goose.

Within a few minutes, Teddy saw the other children in the neighborhood leave their houses and form two groups. One group began playing tag while the other group played dodge ball. Since he didn't want to miss playing either game, Teddy quickly ran into the kitchen where his mother was washing the breakfast dishes.

"Can I play, too?" Teddy asked his mother.

"Yes, Teddy," his mother replied.

Not wasting any time, Teddy raced toward the front door.

"Don't run, Teddy! Walk, please," Teddy's mother shouted as she followed behind him to the door. Then she unlocked the door and stood in the

doorway watching Teddy as he hurried to join the other children.

Teddy first tried the group of children who were playing freeze tag.

"Can I play, too?" he asked the children.

Instead of giving Teddy an answer, the children laughed and pointed at his braces. They also called him names like *robot, four legs, lead foot, and tin man*.

The children's cruel laughter really hurt Teddy's feelings. So he walked away while they continued laughing and playing their game of tag.

Still determined, Teddy tried the other children playing dodge ball.

"Can I play, too?" he asked.

Again, the children laughed at Teddy's braces. This time, the cruel laughter brought tears to Teddy's eyes. He quickly ran home to his sisters, who were watching him from the front porch.

Teddy spent the remainder of the day inside the house. He no longer desired to play outside with the other children. Instead, feeling very unhappy, he watched the other children play from his front window.

Teddy's unhappiness saddened the hearts of his two sisters. Since Loran and Magi were responsible for watching over Teddy while their mother spent most of the day working to support the family, they were very determined to make their little brother feel better.

Later that day, Loran and Magi tried a couple of things they thought would take away Teddy's disappointment and forget the cruel neighborhood children. They tried feeding him chocolate cake and vanilla ice cream because they knew that the two treats always brought a smile to his face. However, Teddy ate neither the ice cream nor the cake.

Then Loran and Magi tried making Teddy feel happy by reading his favorite book to him. Still, the book could not bring a smile to Teddy's sorrowful face. Because Loran and Magi were unable to make Teddy feel happy, they tucked him into bed early that night.

The next morning, Loran and Magi arose very early. They quickly got dressed and headed into town before Teddy could awaken. Their intentions were to buy something truly special. That something special had to make Teddy feel happy. Therefore, Loran and Magi put their heads together to come up with an idea for that special something.

"Let's buy Teddy a football," Loran suggested.

"Yeah, a football," Magi agreed.

Loran and Magi took what little money they had and went to a store that sold sporting goods. They had just enough money to buy a brand new football. Therefore, the store clerk placed the football into a large, plastic shopping bag and handed it to Loran. Then Loran and Magi left the store and hurried home.

Teddy had just finished eating breakfast with his mother when Loran and Magi returned home with the large shopping bag. Teddy watched eagerly as Loran reached into the shopping bag and pulled out the brand new ball.

"Can I play, too?" Teddy asked with a bright look on his baby face.

"Yes, after you brush your teeth and change into your play clothes," Loran answered.

After Teddy got dressed, he and his two sisters went into their backyard to play catch with his new football.

Loran started the game of catch by throwing a swift pass. Teddy tried catching the pass but was unsuccessful. Instead, he was knocked to the ground because the football was almost half his size.

With a smirk on her face, Magi picked Teddy and the football off the ground. She then tossed the ball back to Loran and brushed off the dirt from Teddy's pants with her hands. Loran waited for Teddy to get

into position to receive another pass. However, Teddy positioned himself cautiously because he was afraid of being knocked over again.

"Don't throw it real hard, okay?" Teddy requested before he allowed Loran to throw the next pass.

When Teddy was finally set, Loran threw a much softer pass for him to catch. Again, Teddy tried catching the football, but was unsuccessful. This time, the football bounced off his chest because his eyes were shut.

"Keep your eyes open," Loran instructed.

"You can catch it," added Magi.

"I can't," Teddy cried.

"Just try really hard," replied Loran.

Again, Magi picked up the football and tossed it back to Loran. Teddy got himself ready for Loran's third pass.

Trying hard to keep his eyes open, Teddy caught the third pass from Loran. A big smile crept across his face because he felt so good about catching it. His huge smile was a sign to Loran and Magi that he felt happy again. But to make sure that Teddy was truly feeling happy, Loran shouted, "Let's go inside and celebrate with some chocolate cake and vanilla ice cream!"

"Okay!" Teddy exclaimed.

Aggressively, Teddy spiked the football down to the ground as if he were celebrating a touchdown he had just scored.

"Last one in the house is a rotten egg!" Magi cried. Quickly, Loran, Magi and Teddy raced into the house for some cake and ice cream.

Chapter 4

Teddy's first day of school was less than a day away. Although he wouldn't be five years old for three more weeks, he could still attend kindergarten. Despite being old enough, Teddy did not want to go to school. He feared that the other children would laugh at the braces on his legs. However, he was willing to give school a chance because it was the place where Loran and Magi went each morning. Teddy thought that his sisters could protect him from the other children's laughter.

"Mommy, can Loran and Magi hold my hand at school?" he asked.

"No, Teddy, they won't be in your class," his mother answered.

"I don't wanna go," Teddy cried.

"You must attend school," his mother replied.

"Why?" questioned Teddy.

"Because school is a place where children learn to read and write and play many games," his mother explained.

"Can I play, too?" Teddy asked.

Knowing that playing was very important to Teddy, his mother nodded her head and gave him a huge smile. She then kissed him on the forehead and tucked him into bed.

"Night-night, Mommy," Teddy whispered before closing his eyes to sleep.

The next morning, Teddy tried hiding under the blankets so he didn't have to go to school. He could hear Loran and Magi singing to the music on the radio as they got dressed. Singing was their usual way to get ready for school. However, Teddy was not in the singing mood. He'd rather stay home and watch the morning cartoons. Nevertheless, his mother managed to get him dressed for school.

The morning was windy and cool as Teddy and his mother walked to school. Their walk would be quite long because the school was about a mile away. During the walk, Teddy's mother gave him some precise instructions.

"Wait for Loran to pick you up after school," she said.

Teddy did not respond because his thoughts were

only about playing. After twenty-five minutes of walking, Teddy and his mother finally reached the school. Teddy was overwhelmed by the number of children attending school. In fact he felt that his chances on finding someone to play with were great. Therefore, he began laughing and skipping.

When Teddy and his mother entered the kindergarten classroom, they were approached by a petite young woman who looked slightly over thirty years old. She had short, sandy brown hair and was wearing a blue dress with white polka-dots. The knee high dress was laced with the smell of sweet perfume. The young women was Teddy's teacher.

"Hello, my name is Miss Plum and what is your name?" the teacher asked in greeting Teddy and his mother.

"This is Teddy," Teddy's mother replied.

Then, with a shy look on his face, Teddy greeted Miss Plum.

"Hello," he said politely.

"Nice to meet you, Teddy," replied Miss Plum.

She then took Teddy by the hand and led him to his place in the classroom. The other children stared in amazement at the braces on Teddy's legs as he walked across the room. Teddy was glad to see that the children did not laugh at his braces.

Miss Plum's classroom remained fairly quiet and in order as she taught the first day's lessons to the children. However, when play time came, the children laughed and skipped as they headed outside for the school playground, which was filled with swings, slides, jumping ropes and many types of balls.

Because the playground had so much, every child in Miss Plum's class played – except for Teddy. Instead, he stood against the school wall and watched. He was afraid of being rejected by the children.

But since it was play time, Miss Plum instructed Teddy to play with the other children. Hesitantly, he began walking toward the playground.

As Teddy walked around the playground, he came across four boys playing tag. Since the boys were having so much fun, Teddy decided that he would join them.

"Can I play, too?" he asked the four boys.

Two of the four boys stopped running when they heard Teddy's question.

"No!" yelled the first boy.

"You can't catch us, anyhow," the second boy added.

Then the two boys ran quickly off and rejoined the others. Teddy wanted to cry because he was left alone. Instead, he walked away looking very sad.

As he continued the walk around the playground, Teddy came across a group of girls jumping rope.

"Can I play, too?" he politely asked the girls.

"No!" screamed the girl who was jumping in the middle of the rope.

"Yo funny legs gonna trip on the rope," added the girl who was turning one end of the rope.

Every girl in the group began laughing. Tears fell from Teddy's dejected face as he walked away with his head down. Not feeling any sympathy for the way they had treated Teddy, the girls waved good-bye and continued jumping rope.

Again, Teddy continued walking around the playground until he came across the swings. He decided to stop there because it was the only place on the playground where the other children weren't playing. Teddy simply wanted to be alone.

As Teddy sat on the swing, he sobbed for a brief moment. He then dried his eyes with his hands and tried swinging himself back and forth. He was unsuccessful. Seeing that Teddy was having a very hard time swinging, Miss Plum walked over and gave him a push.

With a half smile on his face, Teddy asked, "Why won't they play with me?"

Miss Plum thought for a second before answer-

ing Teddy's question. "Teddy, you are a special and wonderful little boy. The other children can't understand that now. But one day, you'll have many friends that will play with you and like you for you," she replied.

"Do you like me?" Teddy asked.

"You are one of my favorite students," Miss Plum whispered as she winked her eye.

"Will you be my friend and play with me?" Teddy asked.

"Anytime, Teddy… Anytime," Miss Plum said with a grin, as she pushed him higher on the swing.

When play time was over, Miss Plum lifted Teddy off the swing.

"Let's go inside for some cookies and milk!" she shouted to all the children in the playground. At that point, Teddy took Miss Plum by the hand and laughed and skipped as they joined the other children.

Chapter 5

A couple of days before the next school year, Teddy made another visit to the doctor's office. This time, he was very eager to see Dr. Crisby because he was there to have the braces on his legs removed. Having the braces removed would be the perfect gift for his sixth birthday, which was only three weeks away.

Teddy was excited about having the braces off because it meant that the other children wouldn't have any reason to laugh or tease him. For that reason alone, he didn't need Nurse Sharon to bribe him with a red lollipop to see Dr. Crisby. Nevertheless, Teddy took the red lollipop and allowed Dr. Crisby to remove the braces.

Although wearing the braces for the past three years made Teddy's legs straight as an arrow, his first steps without them were very awkward. Without the braces, he could not keep his toes from turning slightly inward, thus causing him to walk pigeon-toed.

To correct this unique pigeon-toes walk, Dr. Crisby instructed Teddy to practice walking with his toes straight. Not wasting any time to practice, Teddy tried keeping his toes straight as he and his mother walked out of the doctor's office.

The next day, Teddy and his mother hurried to school. They were slightly late because Teddy had to change his shirt after spilling orange juice on it. He simply couldn't wear the orange juice stained shirt to his first grade class.

During the walk to school, Teddy's mother gave him a small reminder.

"Remember to keep your toes straight every time you walk today," she said.

"Okay, Mommy," Teddy replied.

However, Teddy had a very hard time walking with his toes straight while at the same time trying to keep up with his mother's pace. Therefore, his mother placed him on her back and carried him for the remainder of their trip to school.

When they finally arrived at Teddy's classroom, the door was open but the other children were already seated at their desks. Teddy and his mother stood quietly in the doorway while the teacher called out the names from the attendance list.

The teacher read every name on the list except the last one. Pausing for a brief second, the teacher looked over to Teddy and his mother and in a very firm tone called out the last name on the list.

"Theodore Watts!"

"Present," Teddy answered politely.

"Please, you may call him Teddy," his mother explained.

"Okay, Teddy, please have a seat," replied the teacher.

Teddy's mother waved good-bye while Teddy hung his jacket in the coat closet and took a seat. The teacher closed the door and proceeded to the front of the classroom.

"Good morning, my name is Mrs. Hettigrove," the teacher stated to the class as she wrote her name on the chalkboard.

Mrs. Hettigrove was an elderly woman who wore thick, brown framed bifocals. Her breath always had the smell of cough medicine and her clothes were laced with the scent of fresh moth balls. Mrs. Hettigrove never smiled because she would take out her false teeth and place them in a clear glass jar located on her desk. She did this to make sure that she had all of the children's attention. As a result, most of

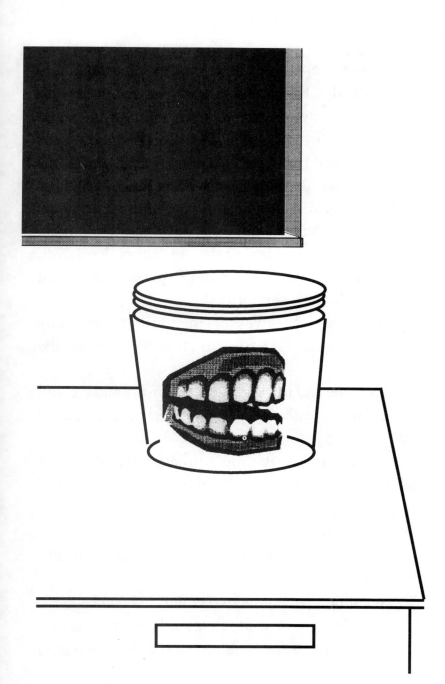

the children were afraid of her.

Inside Mrs. Hettigrove's classroom, Teddy's desk was located between two boys. Peter Slim was seated on Teddy's left side and Paul Slim was seated on his right. Peter and Paul were identical twins who were a year older than all the other children in the class. They were older because they were repeating the first grade.

Neither Peter nor Paul enjoyed doing schoolwork, but they did enjoy playing during recess. However, to play during recess, Peter and Paul both knew that they must do their schoolwork.

Peter, who was always trying to figure out a way to avoid doing any schoolwork, tapped Teddy on the shoulder.

"Give me and my brother the answers and we will be yer friends and play witcha," Peter demanded of Teddy.

Because Teddy was much smaller than the twins and wanted some friends to play with, he agreed to Peter's demand.

"Okay," he replied.

It was 9:00 when Mrs. Hettigrove started teaching class.

"What does one plus two equal?" she asked.

Mrs. Hettigrove waited patiently for an answer. However, none of the children raised their hands to answer the question. Therefore, she called on Peter.

Not knowing the answer, Peter looked over to Teddy for some help. Teddy remembered the deal that he made with Peter.

"Three," he whispered to Peter, hoping that Mrs. Hettigrove would not hear him.

But Mrs. Hettigrove heard Teddy's whisper and became very angry.

"Please have a seat in the corner, Teddy!" she raved.

Teddy sat in the corner of the classroom facing the wall while Mrs. Hettigrove continued teaching the rest of the class.

Soon it was time for recess. All the children in the classroom were allowed to play outside, except for Teddy. He remained sitting in the corner.

Looking out of the classroom window, Teddy could see the other children playing..

"Can I play, too?" he asked Mrs. Hettigrove, who stayed behind as well.

"You may not, Teddy," she answered.

Disappointed with her response, Teddy placed his head down and began sobbing. After five minutes of sobbing, Teddy lifted his head and dried his eyes with his hands.

"Can I play too?" he asked Mrs. Hettigrove for

the second time.

"Yes, Teddy," Mrs. Hettigrove nodded, because she felt that he'd spent enough time inside.

With a huge smile on his face, Teddy jumped out of his seat and raced out the classroom door to join the other children.

"Please slow down, Teddy!" Mrs. Hettigrove shouted.

When Teddy reached the playground, he saw Peter and Paul running. Teddy rushed over to the two boys.

"Can I play, too?" he asked.

Both Peter and Paul stopped running.

"Sure," said Peter.

"Yer it," Paul said as he tagged Teddy.

Quickly, Peter and Paul ran toward the open field. Grinning from ear to ear, Teddy chased after the twins.

As Teddy chased Peter and Paul, he remembered what his mother told him earlier about walking straight. So, he began following his mother's instructions. Although it was very hard for him to run and keep his toes straight, Teddy ran as fast as he could. But it was not fast enough to keep up with Peter and Paul.

Since Teddy could not catch up, Peter and Paul stopped running. They instead picked up a red rubber ball and played catch.

It took a few seconds for Teddy to finally catch up to Peter and Paul.

"Can I play, too?" Teddy asked.

"Sure," said Peter.

Teddy stood between Peter and Paul. Then Paul threw the red ball up in the air for grabs. All three boys tried catching it.

After many attempts to catch the ball, Teddy was unsuccessful. He was simply too short to outreach Peter's and Pauls' long arms. For that reason, Teddy became very discouraged and walked away from the game of catch.

When Teddy was a few paces away, Peter and Paul stopped playing catch and began whispering to each other. They whispered for a minute and then approached Teddy, who was sitting alone under a tall maple tree.

"We're 'bout to play hide and seek," Paul said.

Wiping the tears from eyes, Teddy asked, **"Can I play, too?"**

"Sure, you hide and we'll find yer," Paul replied.

Not wasting any time, Teddy ran far away from the two boys and hid behind a tall rosebush. He positioned himself so that no one could see him. Peter and Paul laughed because they didn't have any intentions of finding Teddy.

Just then, Mrs. Hettigrove shouted for all the children to return to class because recess was over. All the children, except for Teddy, quickly returned back to class. Teddy was too far away to see or hear Mrs. Hettigrove.

It started raining after the other children were safely inside the school. Teddy, who was still hiding behind the rosebush, got soaking wet. With his clothes soaked from the rain, Teddy was forced to come out of hiding.

When Teddy came out from behind the rosebush, he realized that the other children had already gone inside. At that moment, his heart dropped and his face turned pale. He knew that Mrs. Hettigrove would be angry, so he raced toward the school.

As he increased his pace with each stride, Teddy tripped and fell into a mud puddle. With his mouth full of mud, he quickly got up and wiped the mud from his face with his hand. He then continued running toward the school.

Entering Mrs. Hettigrove's classroom, Teddy's face and clothes were covered with mud. It was a wonder that he could see or walk. The other children laughed at his muddy appearance. However, Mrs. Hettigrove did not see any humor in the way Teddy looked.

"Let's go to the principal's office, Teddy!" Mrs. Hettigrove exclaimed as she took Teddy by the hand and walked him out of the classroom.

Teddy was in trouble because the other boys didn't try to find him. He realized that Peter and Paul were not good friends after all.

Chapter 6

During a rainy day in the last week of September, Teddy, along with his mother and Magi, celebrated his ninth birthday. The celebration occurred in the dining room, which was filled with colorful balloons, party decorations and birthday presents. Teddy's mother and sister sang Happy Birthday as Teddy stared at the nine burning candles on the top of his round, two-layered, chocolate covered birthday cake.

"Make a wish and blow out the candles!" Teddy's mother instructed.

Teddy did not have to think long about his birthday wish. There was only one thing that came into his mind.

"I wish Loran were here, too," he thought to himself, before he blew out all nine candles.

The reason for Loran's absence was quite excusable. Earlier that year, she got married and moved to

a different town. Since the town was nearly three hours away by train, Loran had a tough time making it home for Teddy's birthday party.

Teddy wanted his birthday wish to come true because he missed Loran and all the good times they had together, running, laughing and playing in their backyard. Teddy was very close to Loran because she was the only person that could make him happy when he was feeling sad. Without a doubt, Loran was Teddy's best friend in addition to being his oldest sister.

After Teddy finished blowing out the candles, Magi handed him a birthday present. Just as he began opening it, the telephone rang. Magi skipped off to the kitchen to answer the call.

"Hello?" Magi answered. When she found out who was on the other end of the telephone, Magi shouted toward the dining room.

"It's Loran and she wants to talk with the birthday boy!" she exclaimed at the top of her lungs.

Teddy stopped opening his birthday presents and joyfully raced into the kitchen. When he got to the telephone, he was slightly out of breath.

"Hi, Loran," Teddy said with a huge grin.

"Happy birthday, Teddy!" Loran responded.

The sound of Loran's voice sent tears running down Teddy's narrow face. He paused for a brief second to dry his eyes with his hands before continuing the conversation.

"I miss you, Loran," Teddy cried in a sorrowful tone.

Before Loran could tell him about the good news that she had, Teddy handed the telephone back to Magi. Then he dashed back into the dining room to finish opening the rest of his birthday presents. Magi talked with Loran to hear about the news.

Later that night, Teddy said his prayers before tucking himself into bed. While lying in bed, he quietly thought about Loran's good news that Magi had told him. Loran was going to have a baby and Teddy was really excited.

"I hope it's a boy," he thought to himself before he closed his eyes and fell into a deep sleep.

The next morning, Teddy jumped out of bed when he heard his alarm clock buzzing. He felt good and thought that since he was nine years old, he should pick out his own clothes to wear to school, fix his own bowl of cereal for breakfast and walk to school without his mother. Today, Teddy was determined to do all three.

Before breakfast, Teddy washed his face and brushed his teeth.

I'm nine years old, Teddy thought as he took a

long stare into the bathroom mirror. He was looking for some facial hairs that might have grown overnight on his baby face. However, Teddy's face was still hairless.

After breakfast, Teddy decided to ask his mother if he could walk to school alone.

"Can I walk to school by myself?" he asked.

When Teddy's mother first heard the question, she was not fond of the idea. She felt that Teddy was much too young to walk alone. But after giving it a second thought, she decided to allow it because she wanted him to be responsible and independent.

"Remember to look both ways before crossing the street and don't talk to strangers," Teddy's mother instructed. These were the usual instructions mothers gave their children.

At 8:15 a.m., Teddy left the house feeling extremely proud about walking alone to school. He only walked a couple of blocks when something amazing caught his eye. On the sidewalk was an old twenty dollar bill.

At first, Teddy could not believe what he was seeing. The sight of the money was like a dream. Yet, to make sure that he was not dreaming, Teddy closed his eyes. When he opened them again, the money was still there.

"I'm rich!" he shouted with joy.

Teddy then looked around to see if anyone was watching. After he was sure that nobody would see him, Teddy picked up the money. He folded the bill and placed it in his left pocket. Keeping his hand in that same pocket, Teddy skipped to school.

After school, Teddy decided to make a detour through town. There, he could buy something wonderful with the money that he'd found.

When Teddy got into town, he was overwhelmed at the view. The town had many shops, corner stores and restaurants. It also had huge signs and tall buildings that filled the sky. The loud streets were busy with people and cars.

Teddy walked into the first store that he came to. There, he bought some candy and baseball cards, a comic book and a soda pop with the twenty dollar bill. Buying these items left him with very little money. However, Teddy quickly drank down the soda pop and placed the other items into his yellow backpack. Then he took the rest of the money and played arcade games.

After spending all of the money, Teddy left the store and continued his walk through town. As he walked down the street, Teddy heard some loud voices coming from a building ahead of him. The loud building had a big sign in the front window that read:

CENTER STREET BILLIARDS

Teddy was curious. He enter the building to learn why it was so noisy. When he was inside, Teddy had a very difficult time seeing. The lights were very dim and the room was filled with many people who were smoking and playing pool.

Looking around the smoky room, Teddy could only see a gentleman who wore a patch over his left eye. The gentleman was playing alone at the pool table, nearest the exit door. Since the man was alone, Teddy carefully walked up to the gentleman.

"Can I play, too?" Teddy asked.

The gentleman dropped his pool stick on the table and blew smoke from his cigar.

"Yer too young, boy," he stated.

"But I'm nine years old," Teddy insisted.

Because the gentleman found humor in the response, he patted Teddy over the head and snickered.

"What's yer name, boy?" asked the gentleman.

"Theodore Watts. But you can call me Teddy," Teddy replied.

Then the gentleman snickered for a second time and began telling a story.

"*Well, my friends call me Left Eye because I wear this patch on my left eye. I got the patch when I was about your age.*

"*One day, I took my pony named Pearl for a ride off my grandfather's farm. We rode through some woods and across a small creek. After crossing the creek, I saw a huge cave. I rode up for a closer look. As I approached the cave, it began raining very hard, so I went inside to stay warm and dry.*

"*Inside the cave, I sat and rested on a large rock, but before I could get comfortable, a huge black bear started charging towards me. When I saw the bear, I was very scared and couldn't move.*

"*The bear came near me and scratched my left eye with its claw. The pain from the scratch caused me to run as fast as I could out of the cave and onto Pearl's back. We then rode off as fast as we could until the bear was far away.*

"*Today I wear a patch because I still have the bear claw stuck in my left eye,*" the gentleman said, concluding his story.

After hearing the story, Teddy had a startled look upon his face.

"Wow!" he shouted.

Seeing that Teddy was overwhelmed from his story, the gentleman asked, "Do yer want to see the bear claw under my patch, boy?"

"Okay," Teddy answered.

Then the gentleman leaned over. He told Teddy to lift up the patch on his left eye to see the bear claw. Teddy carefully lifted the patch . . . .

"GROWL!!" the gentleman shouted and a very frightened Teddy dropped the patch.

Teddy ran out the door as fast as he could. He did not stop or look back until he was far from the building.

When Teddy finally arrived home, his mother was waiting anxiously at the front door. She was very glad to see him even though he was over an hour late. Instead of giving him a scolding, Teddy's mother gave him a kiss and a huge bear hug. Teddy was glad to see his mother was not upset and he returned her affection with a warm smile.

Chapter 7

The day was extremely hot when Teddy was playing in the backyard. He was visiting his sister Loran and her one year old son, Andrew, Jr., whose nickname was *Ajay*. Teddy had just under two months to spend with Loran and Ajay before he had to return home and start the sixth grade.

Teddy always enjoyed spending his summer vacation with his two sisters. Yet, he would miss Magi this summer because she had left home to attend college.

The day grew hotter as Teddy and Ajay played in the backyard. Ajay sat on the freshly cut lawn, watching Teddy toss a baseball. Teddy was showing Ajay how to catch a baseball the same way his sisters taught him. Teddy loved playing with Ajay. It made him feel like an older brother.

"Keep your eyes open and on the ball," Teddy

explained to Ajay, as he tossed the baseball into the air and caught it as it came down.

Written on the baseball, in big red letters was the name *TEDDY*. The baseball was a gift from Loran on his tenth birthday.

Teddy continued to dazzle Ajay with the height he could toss the baseball. However, on Teddy's next toss, the baseball slipped out of his hand and sailed over the wooden fence.

CRASH!!

The ball broke through a glass window of the big house next door. The loud sound from the glass breaking caused Ajay to start crying. Teddy stood motionless for a brief second as his heart began beating faster than usual. Then, in a state of panic, Teddy picked up Ajay and hurried the two of them into Loran's house.

An hour passed before Teddy thought about telling Loran what had happened. He knew that it was wrong to hide from his mistake. He also knew that he had to tell Loran and go next door to apologize for the accident. Besides, this was the only way to get his baseball back.

After telling Loran what had happened, Teddy left the house to apologize and retrieve his ball. As he walked to the house next door, he had second thoughts about going. Scary images about the person living

there flooded his mind and made him slightly afraid to complete his journey. He imagined a ten foot tall man who weighed nearly a ton. Even a big, mean dog who didn't like little boys seemed quite logical to him. In spite of all the scary thoughts, Teddy knew that he had to go because he wanted his baseball back.

As Teddy walked closer to the house next door, his pace decreased and his heart rate increased. He felt like turning around and trying again tomorrow.

"Maybe nobody's home," Teddy mumbled as he walked up the porch stairs. "The only way to find out is to ring the doorbell."

At that point, his pace was as slow as a snail's crawl. The porch floor made a creaking sound as he approached the front door. Stopping in front of the door, he tried peeking through the large keyhole. Unable to see anything, Teddy swallowed and took his right hand out of his shorts pocket to ring the doorbell. However, before he could ring the bell, a red fire truck drove by with its loud siren sounding off. The startling sound from the siren caused Teddy to jump back from the door.

When Teddy realized that it was only a fire truck, he took a deep breath and approached the door for the second time. This time, he managed to push the doorbell.

A minute passed and no one answered the door. Teddy was quite relieved that no one had answered. Therefore, he decided to leave and try again tomorrow. But, before he could get halfway down the porch stairs, the door slowly opened. So he turned around cautiously to see who, or what, was opening the door.

When the door opened completely, three furry cats pranced out. Close behind the cats, an elderly woman appeared in the doorway.

"You must be Teddy," the elderly woman said as she held Teddy's baseball in her wrinkled hand.

With a very surprised look on his face, Teddy nodded his head and took another deep swallow. He wondered how she knew his name, not thinking just then that the woman had simply read his name from the baseball.

"This must be yours," the woman said as she handed over the baseball. "I've been waiting for you."

"I'm sorry for breaking your window," Teddy tried explaining. "It was an accident."

"Well, sorry can't fix my broken window," the woman replied.

Teddy felt very embarrassed and truly sorry about breaking the woman's window.

"Do you have any money to fix it?" the woman asked.

"No," answered Teddy truthfully.

"Well, you can begin working for me tomorrow to pay for it. I will expect you early tomorrow after you have eaten breakfast," the woman explained.

"Okay," replied Teddy as he started to turn away and walk back down the porch stairs. But before he could take a step, she spoke again.

"By the way, my name is Mrs. Zura, and be sure to wear some old clothes tomorrow," the old woman shouted down to Teddy before she closed the door.

Early the next morning, Teddy rang the doorbell to Mrs. Zura's house. This time, it only took her a few seconds to answer the door.

"Meet me in the backyard," she said.

When Teddy went to the backyard, Mrs. Zura had a paintbrush and some white paint.

"Can you paint, Teddy?" Mrs. Zura asked.

"I don't know," Teddy replied.

"Well, I want you to whitewash the fence," Mrs. Zura ordered.

Teddy didn't bother to ask her how. He just took the brush and began painting the dirty wooden fence.

"Good luck, Teddy," Mrs. Zura stated as words for encouragement. Then she went into her house.

After a couple of hours, Mrs. Zura returned with a tray of sandwiches, a bag of potato chips and a pitcher of ice water. It was lunchtime and Teddy was still painting the fence. His sweaty face had white paint all over it.

"Lunchtime," Mrs. Zura shouted.

Without any hesitation, Teddy stopped painting and rushed toward the lunch tray. He was very hungry from the hard work. Therefore, he didn't bother to say much other than "Thank you" before eating.

As Teddy ate lunch, Mrs. Zura admired her newly painted fence that was half finished. Thus far, Teddy had done a fine job even though it was his first time painting. Mrs. Zura wanted to complement Teddy on the good job he'd done. However, she didn't bother to disturb him because he was enjoying his lunch. Instead, she remained quiet and soaked up some of the warm sun.

After Teddy was finished eating, he sat on the grass with a look of contentment. Mrs. Zura took the lunch tray back into the house. Teddy's feelings toward Mrs. Zura were mixed.

On one hand, he thought that she was a very mean and bitter old lady who loved having children work hard. On the other hand, he felt that she was a very sweet woman who gave his ball back and made him a very nice lunch. Teddy thought about Mrs. Zura for only a brief moment before he fell asleep.

About ten minutes into Teddy's nap, Mrs. Zura returned. This time, she had a baseball and a leather catcher's glove. She began playing catch with herself by tossing the ball up into the air. The sound of the ball hitting the leather glove woke Teddy from his nap.

When Teddy opened his eyes, he saw Mrs. Zura playing catch.

"Can I play, too?" he asked.

"Perhaps when you get done painting the fence," Mrs. Zura replied.

With a huge smirk on his face, Teddy rushed over to the fence and began painting. Mrs. Zura stopped playing catch because she didn't want to distract Teddy from his work. Instead, she returned back into the house with the ball and glove.

After three long hours, Teddy finished painting Mrs. Zura's wooden fence. He was very tired and his arms were sore. With his sleepy face completely covered with white paint, Teddy was simply too exhausted to play catch. So, he asked Mrs. Zura if he could go home instead.

"Can I go home now?" Teddy asked.

"Yes, Teddy," Mrs. Zura called through the screen door.

With the satisfied feeling of having done a good

job, Teddy started on his short walk home. However, before he could get out of the backyard, Mrs. Zura shouted through the screen door once more.

"Come back tomorrow because I have one more job for you," she said.

Teddy was just too tired to respond.

The next morning, Teddy sat at the kitchen table eating his breakfast at a turtle's pace. Today he wanted to play with Ajay instead of working for Mrs. Zura. Nevertheless, Teddy finished his breakfast and walked over to her house.

When Teddy got to the house, the garage door was open. Inside, Mrs. Zura was sitting in her old black car.

HONK! HONK!

She blew the horn for Teddy to come inside the garage.

Although Mrs. Zura's car was in excellent condition, it was extremely dirty. The car needed to be washed and waxed. So, Mrs. Zura drove her car out of the garage for Teddy to wash and wax. Again, Teddy didn't have much experience in washing and waxing cars. His only experience was watching a couple of older boys about a year ago. But, he did not bother to tell Mrs. Zura anything different.

"Good luck, Teddy," Mrs. Zura said, giving him

those same words for encouragement.

After two hours, when Teddy finished putting a coat of wax on the car, Mrs. Zura returned with a tray of lunch. Her timing was right because Teddy's stomach was growling from being hungry and thirsty. This time, Mrs. Zura had ice cream along with a couple of sandwiches and a bag of potato chips. Since it was extremely hot, Teddy ate the ice cream before devouring the sandwiches and potato chips. Besides, ice cream was one of his favorite foods.

After lunch, Teddy buffed the coat of wax off the car. The car shined as bright as the sun. He was very proud of the job that he'd done. Mrs. Zura was very pleased as well. As a result, Teddy saw Mrs. Zura smile for the first time.

Since Mrs. Zura's old black car looked good as new, she informed Teddy that he had worked enough to pay for her broken window. She also invited him to come back tomorrow afternoon for a ride in her car. Teddy graciously accepted her offer and skipped home.

The next day, Teddy anxiously waited for the afternoon to arrive. He was eager to go on the ride that Mrs. Zura had promised.

Maybe she can teach me how to drive, Teddy thought to himself.

After lunch, Teddy hurried over to Mrs. Zura's house. When he got there, Mrs. Zura was pulling up to the driveway in her old, shiny black car.

HONK! HONK!

She blew the horn for Teddy to get inside the car. Not wasting any time, Teddy hopped in and closed the door behind him. Mrs. Zura gave him a wink of her eye and quickly drove off.

As Mrs. Zura drove through the busy streets, Teddy didn't bother to ask her where they were headed. Instead, he buckled his seat belt and sat back to enjoy the ride. Besides, he didn't have to do any work for her today and that was fine with him.

After thirty minutes of driving, Mrs. Zura pulled into a large parking lot and parked her car. The parking lot was located outside of a huge baseball stadium. Teddy could not understand why they had stopped inside this large parking lot.

"Have you ever been to a professional baseball game, Teddy?" Mrs. Zura asked.

"No," Teddy shook his head.

"Well, here we are," Mrs. Zura said with a devilish grin on her face.

Teddy and Mrs. Zura got out of the car and walked toward the baseball stadium. When they entered the stadium, Mrs. Zura bought some hot dogs and soda

pop for them to eat and drink. Then, they quickly found their seats before the baseball game started.

At the start of the game, Teddy saw nine baseball players with fancy green uniforms run onto the field. He was truly amazed by the way in which they played the game.

"Can I play, too?" Teddy asked.

"Maybe later," Mrs. Zura replied as she winked her eye.

After the game, Mrs. Zura took Teddy into a long tunnel that was guarded by a gentleman who was dressed like a police officer.

"Great game, Mrs. Zura," the gentleman stated as he let Teddy and Mrs. Zura go through the tunnel.

"It sure was," Mrs. Zura replied.

At the end of that tunnel was the baseball field. Teddy hurried onto the field with Mrs. Zura following closely behind.

From ground view, Teddy realized that the field was much bigger than it had looked from his seat. The idea of being on a professional baseball field gave him goose bumps.

Taking an imaginary swing, Teddy imagined hitting a home run and began running around the bases. As he touched home plate, a lean young man came out of the home team's dugout. The young man was a professional baseball player. More importantly, he was Mrs. Zura's son.

The young man walked over to Mrs. Zura and gave her a hug and a kiss.

"Hello, mom," he greeted.

"This is Teddy, the little boy I told you about," Mrs. Zura replied.

"Well, hello, Teddy," the young man said, as he handed Teddy a baseball and a glove.

"Can I play, too?" Teddy asked with a gleam in his eyes.

Seeing that Teddy was excited about the ball and glove, the young man nodded his head and began playing catch with him. Then, Mrs. Zura gave Teddy those same words for encouragement.

"Good luck, Teddy," she said.

It turned out to be one of the most exciting days of his young life.

Chapter 8

Teddy was starting seventh grade in a week. He and his mother had moved to the next town to a nice, two-bedroom apartment. They didn't need the large space from their old house because Loran and Magi had left home. Since Teddy had very few friends in his old town and school, he didn't mind moving. Perhaps he could make some new friends.

After moving into the apartment, Teddy decided to take a walk through the neighborhood. As Teddy walked, he discovered a large park that was only a couple of blocks away from the apartment complex.

The park was a beautiful place because it contained many cornerstones with long benches where people could sit and relax. It also had many swings, slides and sandboxes where little children could laugh and play. Although the long benches, swings, slides and sandboxes looked extremely nice, Teddy did not find them interesting. What he did find interesting from afar were the smooth blacktop basketball courts. Drawn by the sounds of the games being played there, Teddy walked over to the basketball courts for a closer look.

When Teddy entered the court area, he saw boys, who were much taller than he, playing a pick up game of basketball. Although they looked to be about his age, the height of the boys intimidated Teddy. Therefore, he just stood quietly and watched the game.

When the game was over, the tallest boy on the court began picking two new teams. The excitement from the previous game made Teddy forget that he was intimidated by the much taller boys. Instead, he wanted to play with them.

"Can I play, too?" Teddy asked.

"No, you're too short," replied the boy who was picking the two teams.

Teddy did not bother to argue with the boy. He just turned and walked away.

As Teddy walked with his head down, he heard a squeaky voice from the next court.

"You can play with me, if you wanna," said the voice.

Teddy lifted his head and saw another boy who was standing alone with an old basketball underneath

his left arm. The boy took four dribbles with the old ball and began walking toward Teddy. As the boy got closer, Teddy could see that he was extremely tall and slender. Teddy also noticed that the boy walked with a limp.

"Do you play ball?" the boy asked as he handed Teddy his basketball.

Teddy gave a nod and a short grin. Then he dribbled the basketball once before taking a shot toward the basket. *SWISH!*

Teddy made a lucky shot right into the basket. The boy gave Teddy two thumbs up for the successful shot.

"Hey, my name is Dudley June," greeted the boy.

"I'm Teddy Watts," Teddy answered.

Dudley and Teddy shook hands and they began playing basketball.

Dudley June was only a couple of months older than Teddy. From time to time, he'd lose some of the feeling in his right leg, which caused him to walk with a limp. In addition to being the same age and walking with a limp, Dudley lived only a couple of blocks away from the park and Teddy's apartment complex.

After a couple of days of playing basketball together, Teddy and Dudley became very good friends.

Their friendship carried into the next week when school began. Since they were in many of the same classes, Dudley and Teddy became inseparable.

On the fourth day of school, Dudley didn't show up for class. Teddy was curious about Dudley's absence. So, after school, he hurried over to Dudley's house. There, Teddy learned from Dudley's younger sister that Dudley was in the hospital. Quickly, Teddy rushed to the hospital to see his friend.

When Teddy arrived at the hospital, the woman sitting at the front desk directed him to Dudley's room. Teddy knocked twice before opening the door and entering.

Inside the room, Teddy saw Dudley lying in a hospital bed. Dudley's mother was reading a book. The sight of Teddy brought a smile to Dudley's face.

"How was school today?" Dudley asked.

Teddy didn't bother to answer because he was very nervous. Hospitals always made him feel that way. Moreover, seeing Dudley lying in bed didn't ease his nervousness.

Dudley did not have a choice about being in the hospital because early that morning, he lost complete feeling in his right leg. He did not want to tell Teddy this, knowing that it would make his friend more nervous. Instead, he made up a story.

"I got a little cold and the doctor wants me to stay and get some rest," Dudley explained to Teddy.

"I'll be out of here and back to school in a couple of days."

Teddy could only nod his head because he didn't know what to say to his friend. At that moment, a nurse entered the room and informed Teddy that visiting hours were over. Teddy gave Dudley a handshake and said, "Goodbye."

The next day after school, Teddy went back to the hospital to see Dudley. When he got to Dudley's room, he saw a different nurse.

"Where's my friend, Dudley?" he asked the nurse.

"He is in surgery," the nurse answered.

"When can I see him?" Teddy asked politely.

"You'll have to come back at the beginning of next week," replied the nurse.

The news about Dudley's surgery puzzled Teddy. He thought that Dudley only had a small cold and couldn't figure out why surgery was needed. Nevertheless, he followed the nurse's instructions and left the hospital.

At the beginning of the next week, Teddy returned to the hospital. This time, he found that Dudley's room was occupied by a different patient.

"Where's my friend, Dudley?" Teddy asked the

nurse who was attending to the new patient.

"He went home yesterday," the nurse answered.

Teddy was very happy to hear that Dudley went home. He didn't waste any time leaving the hospital and headed straight to Dudley's house.

When Teddy arrived at Dudley's house, he rang the doorbell. Dudley's mother answered the door.

"Hello, Teddy," she greeted.

"Hi, can I see Dudley, ma'am?" Teddy asked.

"You will have to see him tomorrow because he is sleeping now," Dudley's mother replied.

"Please tell him I came by then," requested Teddy.

"Will do, Teddy," Dudley's mother said.

The next day, Teddy went back to Dudley's house. Again, Dudley's mother answered the door. She said she was sorry, but Dudley was sleeping again and couldn't be disturbed.

Teddy tried everyday for an entire week to see Dudley. Still, his attempts resulted in the same way. Not able to see Dudley during or after school was very frustrating for Teddy. It was quite evident that Dudley was avoiding him and didn't want to see him. Therefore, Teddy stopped trying to see his friend.

Each day over the next two weeks, Teddy played basketball alone at the park. However, on the day before his twelfth birthday, Teddy heard a familiar voice as he shot baskets in the park.

"I can play, too!" said the familiar voice.

Hearing the familiar voice, Teddy knew it was Dudley's. So he turned quickly to see his friend.

When Teddy caught a glimpse of Dudley, he was astonished. He dropped his basketball and stared a long time at his friend. Dudley, who was walking with a pair of wooden crutches, had only one leg. Apparently his right leg was removed in surgery during his stay at the hospital.

Teddy continued to stare with a blank look on his face as Dudley walked closer. When Dudley was close enough, he extended his right hand to Teddy. Instead of shaking his friend's hand, Teddy gave his friend a welcoming hug. Dudley returned Teddy's gesture with a half smile.

Chapter 9

The next school year began and Teddy was entering the eighth grade. He'd spent most of his summer vacation playing basketball in the park with Dudley, who was only able to watch because it was hard for him to play on one leg.

Playing in the park over the summer vacation made Teddy very fond of basketball. His fondness went as far as wanting to play for his school's basketball team. Therefore, he decided to try out for the team.

On the day of basketball tryouts, Teddy quietly stood on the court among the taller boys. With thoughts on his mind about making the team, Teddy stretched while the other boys huddled and talked in their small cliques. This lasted until the coaches came onto the court.

At the start of the tryouts, the head coach blew a whistle to get the boys' attention. Then the boys formed a single line in the order that their names were called. Teddy stood at the very end of the line because his name was last. Being last in line simply meant that he would be the last to perform each drill.

The tryouts lasted for two long, exhausting hours. When tryouts were done, every boy, except Teddy, sat along the court sideline to recuperate. Teddy ran laps around the court to impress the coaches who were gathered at the other end of the court to make a final decision on which twelve boys made the team. There were over twenty boys trying out.

When the coaches were finished, they assembled the boys into one large circular group. The head coach stood in the center of the circle and called out the names of the twelve boys who made the team.

Teddy crossed his fingers and held his breath as he listened for his name to be called.

After seven names, Teddy began to worry because his name was not called. He knew that his chances to make the team were slowly slipping away. However, he tried to remain optimistic.

When the next four names were announced, Teddy still didn't hear his name. Sweat poured down his anguished face. He knew that his chance to make the team was very slim because there was only one spot left and over ten boys waiting to be called.

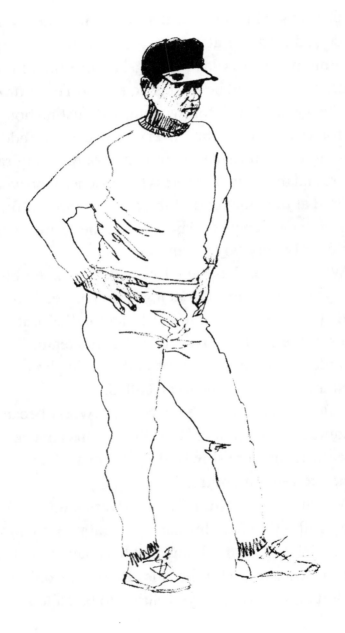

When the last name was called, Teddy realized that it wasn't his. He felt very disappointed and that he'd let down his mother and his friend, Dudley.

"How can I tell them?" Teddy wondered as he watched the boys who made the team celebrate. Then Teddy cleared his mind and gathered up his personal belongings.

Before Teddy could leave the gym, he was approached by the head coach who wanted to speak with him. Teddy could not imagine the reason why the coach would want to talk to him.

Maybe he made a mistake by not calling my name, Teddy thought.

Before another thought could enter Teddy's mind, the head coach smiled and placed his hand on Teddy's shoulder.

"Teddy… my man," the coach blurred.

"Yes, sir?" Teddy responded.

"Please, call me Coach Ben," insisted the coach.

"Okay," Teddy agreed.

"Teddy, I need a boy like you," Coach Ben stated.

"Why?" asked Teddy.

"I need you to work with the team. You'll be our team manager," explained Coach Ben.

Being the team's manager meant that Teddy would be in charge of collecting the basketballs and giving the players water and towels during practices and games. This wasn't the position Teddy had in mind. However, he continued to listen to what Coach Ben was offering.

"You can practice with the team as well. Your hard work and great spirit will motivate the other boys to play well," stated Coach Ben.

When Teddy heard that he could practice with the team, his eyes lit up. Practicing meant that Teddy would be part of the team. Therefore, he didn't bother to give the idea of being the team's manager anymore thought.

"Okay," he agreed.

Since Teddy was allowed to practice, he knew that he could stretch the truth by telling his mother and Dudley that he'd made the team. Neither of them would know the difference unless they came to watch him play. However, Teddy's role would remain a secret because he didn't plan to invite them to any of the games.

After two weeks of practice, the team was ready to play its first game. During the game, Teddy sat on the bench as he watched the team warm up with a lay-up drill. Unlike the boys on the team who were dressed in blue uniforms, Teddy was dressed in his regular clothes.

When the team was finished warming up, Teddy collected all the basketballs and warm-up clothes. He then passed out water bottles. Teddy was reminded of the manager's job when a player from the other team shouted to him, "Hey, ball boy!"

At the start of the game, something caught Teddy's eye. It was his mother and Dudley entering the gymnasium. Their being there was a big surprise, and a major problem. Therefore, before he could be spotted, Teddy quickly grabbed a pair of the team's warm-up suits and put it on to camouflage his regular clothes and his managerial role.

Throughout the game, Teddy tried hiding the fact that he was only the team's manager. However, his role was quite evident when the coaches and players kept giving him direct orders to supply them with water and towels. Besides, Teddy knew that his role will be revealed during halftime when he had to give back the warm-up suit that he was wearing.

After the game, the players and coaches ran into the locker room. Teddy stayed behind to collect the empty water bottles and sweaty towels. His mother and Dudley walked up to congratulate him on the team's win.

"Great game, Teddy!" Dudley exclaimed.

"We're so proud of you," Teddy's mother expressed.

Teddy just nodded his head because he felt bad about not telling them the truth. Therefore, he took a little time out from collecting the empty water bottles and sweaty towels to explain that he had not been completely honest.

After Teddy had explained it all, his mother and friend were still proud. They were also very glad that he had told the truth. Teddy was glad, as well.

During the remainder of the season, the team continued to win. Teddy enjoyed each win just as much as the other boys. In fact, he participated in every victory cheer and celebration.

On the last game of the season, one of the twelve players became very ill and could not show up for the game. That left the team with only eleven players. Coach Ben always liked having twelve players on the bench during each game. Therefore, he decided to let Teddy fill the twelfth spot.

Excited about filling in, Teddy quickly dressed into the team's uniform before Coach Ben could change his mind. Then Teddy stood before the mirror and marveled at his appearance.

I finally made the team, he thought to himself.

Teddy continued to stare into the mirror for a few minutes and dreamt about scoring the team's winning points. His dream was interrupted when Coach Ben shouted, "It's showtime!"

During the game, Teddy sat on the bench next to Coach Ben. As each minute ticked away, Teddy became more anxious to go into the game. He knew that if he remained on the bench, he couldn't make the team's winning shot. Therefore, he needed to get into the game soon.

"Can I play, too?" Teddy asked.

"Not now, Teddy," Coach Ben replied.

Teddy continued watching the game quietly and anxiously from the bench as his team trailed by one point.

When there was only a minute left in the game, Coach Ben called for a time out. They had made a number of baskets and the team was ahead by thirteen points. Knowing that his team had clinched the win, Coach Ben decided to put Teddy into the game.

"Teddy, you're in the game for Gus," Coach Ben said.

Teddy jumped off the bench and sprinted to the score table to check into the game. The fans cheered and chanted, "Teddy, Teddy, Teddy," as he ran onto the court.

During the next fifty seconds, both teams went up and down the court. Teddy didn't get the opportu-

nity to touch the basketball. However, with only nine seconds left in the game, he intercepted a pass from the other team. He then dribbled the ball to the other end of the court as fast as he could. With only two seconds remaining in the game, Teddy took a shot at the basket.

BONG!!

The ball bounced in and out of the basket as the horn sounded for the end of the game. Teddy stared down at the ball with a look of disappointment while his teammates huddled at center court to celebrate their championship win. Only Teddy was disappointed that his shot hadn't gone in.

Chapter 10

During the summer vacation, something strange and amazing happened to Teddy. He grew seven inches in height. Now, he was slightly over six feet tall and going into his freshman year at high school. His classmates began to call him Ted. His mother and sisters continued to call him Teddy, but he was pleased that his friends used a more mature name.

In addition to growing taller, Ted had spent the whole summer practicing extremely hard on the basketball court. He wanted to make the high school freshman boys basketball team. He needed another chance to make a basket since he was still haunted by the shot that he had missed last season.

On the day of basketball tryouts, Ted was very focused and determined to make the team. When it was his turn to perform the drills, Ted dribbled the basketball with amazing speed and quickness. He passed and shot the basketball very accurately. Ted's basketball skills were much improved from the previous year. In fact, he could play just as well as the other boys who were also trying out for the team.

During the next day of school, the list of boys who made the team was posted outside the coach's office. Ted found his name at the top of the list. He felt very excited about making the team. So, he rushed home after school to tell his mother and Dudley the good news.

After two weeks of practice, Ted became one of the five starters on the team. He was also voted one of the team's captains by his teammates and coaches. These two achievements boosted Ted's confidence.

During the season, the team won its first ten games. Ted was the main reason for the team's early success because he scored over half the team's total points. He also excited the many people who came to watch the games with his quick dribbling and accurate shooting. For his success, Ted was promoted to play on the varsity team for the remainder of the season.

After each victory, Ted went out celebrating with his new friends on the team and spent less time at home and with Dudley. Ted's success made him one of the most popular students in high school.

Since Ted was a varsity basketball player, he hung out with the most popular students at the coolest places after school. He was even asked to the senior class prom by a girl in the twelfth grade. Ted was the talk of the school.

Two days before the team's state championship game, the school held a pep rally dance for the boy's varsity basketball team in the gymnasium. Ted was there amongst his new friends and teammates. They were all dancing and having a good time.

Fifteen minutes into the dance, Dudley entered the pep rally. With crutches under his arms, Dudley walked across the gymnasium floor. Every student in the gym stopped dancing and began staring at Dudley.

"Who's that?" one of Ted's teammates whispered.

"That's my buddy, Dudley," Ted answered.

Then Ted raised his right arm and waved to get Dudley's attention. Dudley smiled when he saw Ted waving from the other side of the gymnasium.

"Ted!" Dudley shouted as he hurried across the gym floor.

Ted watched as his friend approached him. However, before Dudley could get halfway across the gym, *CRASH!*

Dudley tripped and fell in the middle of the floor. Everyone, except for Ted, began laughing at Dudley's

fall. Dudley remained helpless on the floor with a look of embarrassment upon his face. Ted ran over to help his friend off the floor.

"Are you okay?" Ted asked as he gave Dudley a hand.

Dudley nodded his head and dusted off his shirt.

"Let's go home... now," Ted suggested.

"No. You belong here and I don't, so I'll go and you stay," replied Dudley.

Dudley slowly turned away and walked out of the gym while the other students continued to laugh. Ted held his head down as his teammates mocked Dudley's fall.

During the next day in school, Ted went to see the head coach of the basketball team. The night before, Ted had decided that he wanted to quit the team. What happened to Dudley at the dance made him realize that he did not fit in with his teammates and his new friends. Therefore, he handed in his uniform.

The coach was astonished that his star player was quitting. But after Ted explained how he felt as a little boy wearing orthopedic braces because of a birth defect. And how it hurt when other children laughed and teased him. And when the night before, when his teammates laughed at the misfortunes of a crippled student, all of the old hurts came back to him. He didn't think his teammates and friends could be that cruel. The coach understood and admired Ted.

In addition to quitting the basketball team, Ted stopped hanging out with the popular students at the coolest places. Instead, he spent the rest of the school year to himself.

In the summer, Ted regained his desire to play basketball. So, every morning he went to the park where he had first started playing. There, he shot baskets alone.

One day, during his usual shoot around at the park, Ted heard a familiar voice behind him.

"I can play, too!" the voice said.

He knew that the voice was from his friend, Dudley. He quickly turned to see him. When Ted turned to see his friend, Dudley was walking without his crutches. Dudley didn't need the crutches because he had a new artificial right leg. Seeing Dudley walking again without his crutches brought a huge smile to Ted's sweaty face.

Without any further delay, Ted passed Dudley the basketball. Dudley caught and shot the ball towards the basket. *SWISH!* The ball went through the hoop.

"I can play, too!" Dudley shouted with joy.

Ted gave Dudley two thumbs up. Then the two friends hugged and began playing basketball together, similar to when they first met years before.

After a few minutes of playing with Dudley, Ted heard more familiar voices behind him. He stopped and turned again. This time, the voices were from his two sisters, Loran and Magi, and his five year old nephew, Ajay.

Overwhelmed by the site of the basketball courts, Ajay asked, **"Can I play, too?"**

Ted looked at Ajay, at his strong, sturdy little legs and he smiled and nodded his head. Then he gently passed the ball to his nephew. Ajay caught the ball and as Ted lifted him high over his head, he shot the ball toward the basket.

SWISH!

AFTERWORDS

This book was written out of the sincere desire to inspire young people to pursue their aspirations. The messages in the story will assist in achieving those aspirations. However, if there are any doubts, take the first two words in the title, *Can I Play, Too?* and switch them around into *I Can.*

VALUABLE MESSAGES FROM
Can I Play, Too?
FOR YOUNG PEOPLE

- *Hiding won't solve a problem that you may be facing.*
- *You shouldn't make fun of others who are different.*
- *You may fall while trying to accomplish a goal, but don't ever quit.*
- *Be very careful about talking to strangers.*
- *Things that look good and safe on the outside may not really be good and safe.*
- *Mistakes are only wrong if you hide them.*
- *Good things can happen when you work hard.*
- *Sometimes, sacrifices must be made to get what you really want.*
- *Just because others are doing wrong doesn't mean that you should join them. After all, two wrong doings don't make a right doing.*

About the Author

The story of Teddy was inspired by K. Scott Conover's childhood experiences and challenges. Like Teddy, Scott had to overcome an early walking problem by wearing orthopedic braces on his legs. He was also laughed at by the other children in his neighborhood and his school and labeled as being different. Many times, Scott was not allowed to "play, too" due to various reasons related to the braces he wore or his size. During his eighth grade year in school, Scott joined the Pop Warner Football team for the first time. He was not allowed to play in any of the team's games because he was over the weight limit. However, he never stopped trying and practiced everyday with the team.

Today, K. Scott Conover is an offensive lineman in the National Football League and played his first six seasons with the Detroit Lions. He was selected by the Lions in the fifth round in 1991 from Purdue University, where he graduated with a bachelor of science degree in Industrial Technology.

In November, 1994, Scott founded the Scott Conover Youth Foundation to ensure perpetual involvement with youths, while subsidizing economically disadvantaged youth in educational and recreational activities. Like the Foundation, Scott hopes that this book will inspire all youth to "play, too."

"Life begins today... One youth at a time."
–The Scott Conover Foundation

Scott sees an opportunity to make a difference

His patience and persistence make him one of the best among the best.

During the off seasons, Scott and his team mates participate in various charitable functions. Here Scott is selling popcorn to a delighted crowd.

On the outside, he looks like a lion, but on
the inside he's a warm Teddy Bear

Scott takes his NFL future into his own hands